HEART
OF
A KILLER

CONNOR WHITELEY

HEART OF A KILLER

No part of this book may be reproduced in any form or by any electronic or mechanical means. Including information storage, and retrieval systems, without written permission from the author except for the use of brief quotations in a book review.

This book is NOT legal, professional, medical, financial or any type of official advice.

Any questions about the book, rights licensing, or to contact the author, please email connorwhiteley@connorwhiteley.net

Copyright © 2021 CONNOR WHITELEY

All rights reserved.

DEDICATION
Thank you to all my readers without you I couldn't do what I Love.

HEART OF A KILLER

It was happening all over again.

Hellen knew that as soon as she walked inside the damp mould covered wooden house with its small box like rooms. Hellen knew exactly where everything was here. From the little kitchen with a broken constantly dripping tap in the back to this main room that served as a living, dining and bedroom.

She frowned a little as she stepped over a mouldy broken plate in the doorway and she went inside further.

Her massive wooden stick tapped gently against the floor that crumbled with each step she took. Kicking up all sort of nasty things into the air.

Hellen took a few more steps as she stood on something that made her foot slimy and wet.

Inspecting the little house, a memory of her playing in here as a child with some of her friends sprang to mind. It was a lot nicer back then and this was a house that wasn't reduced to ruin. How times change.

The sound of the constantly dripping tap still went on in the background as Hellen remembered how disgusting that water tasted all those decades ago.

As she walked to the middle of the little house, she crushed a little toy covered in some sort of dead animal. A rat perhaps? Hellen really didn't want to find out.

The reason was she was here dressed in her grey Procurator coat was because she was an Officer of the Law working for the Queen and someone had randomly decided to end someone. Well that was what the report said.

Yet Hellen didn't remember too many of the details whilst her mind was still a little foggy after last night's... fun with one of the Royal Guards. Those people can move!

The sound of damp mould drew Hellen's focus back to the ruined house. The black mould covered every inch of this disgusting place. Hellen didn't know why the house was still standing. Everyone in Ordericous knew this was a health hazard in an unloved part of the country. Maybe she should throw her weight around and get it destroyed. It might stop a few people from getting sick. Maybe she would.

Turning around Hellen held her grey Procurator cloak over her nose as the air stunk of rotten meat and the sound of the flies buzzing reached her ears.

Looking over at the little dead yellow straw bed in the far corner of the little disgusting room, Hellen found exactly what she thought she would find. A half devoured corpse.

Simply lying there, stretched out on the straw bed for the rats and other foul creatures of the night to devour.

Hellen shook her head.

It was happening all over again.

Stepping carefully over to the corpse and bed, Hellen gagged as the smell of rotten flesh grew stronger and stronger. But thankfully the buzzing of the flies died down. Almost as if Hellen was scaring them.

After all, she had been told on more than one occasion of her scariness.

Standing only a metre away from the corpse, Hellen skilfully used her massive wooden stick to pull the flies and their lava off the victim.

Then Hellen had to frown and a wave of... sadness (she supposed) washed over her. She had seen this all before as she noted the flayed skin on the lower parts of the devoured body. Chunks of his skin still laid there attached to his body.

Moving her eyes up his body, Hellen supposed he must have been a strong lad once. Judging by a couple chunks of strong well defined abs that were barely eaten.

Then the real horror revealed itself. Judging by the saw and dagger marks on his chest, Hellen gave a deep frown as she thought about how the killer had carved out the man's still beating heart. Before making the victim watch his own heart beat whilst the foul killer continued to carve out their organs.

Hellen had to look away from the body.

Her studies at the Procurator academy only went so far. The real reason she sadly knew most of this was because she had seen the killer at work once. So long ago but not long enough.

Hellen walked over to the other side of the room. Listening to the dripping tap in the background and feeling the ruined floor under her feet.

The memory of investigating this killer, eventually finding him and then almost becoming his next victim flashed through her mind.

It was the same killer.

The memories of seeing the poor woman being killed in this horrific way always played in her mind at night. Having plenty of… special exercise helped but it never stopped the memories for long.

Looking over back at the corpse, Hellen made herself take a deep vile breath of this truly horrific damp mouldy air as she focused on this crime.

She might have failed to catch the killer once but not again. She was not going to let him take another life and that was a promise.

***

As Hellen breathed in the thick black smoke around her that left a foul bitter taste in her mouth, she frowned at the immense metal cladded warehouses that stretched back for as far as the eye could see and tens of metres into the sky. Housing all sorts of carriages, workshops and tools needed for repairing ships. Their metal cladding was an assault on the eyes with its ugly grey and rusted look.

Hellen lent against one of the metal cladded warehouses, its cold metal sending chills through her soft Procurator cloak, and she looked around with a frown at this square of open ground surrounded by these warehouses.

She dug the end of her massive wooden stick in the gravel covered ground. Listening to the gravel moan a little amongst the sounds of ships and dockworkers a few hundred metres away. Then the faint sound of waves hitting the edge of the docks tens of metres away reminded Hellen of how unloved this part of the docks were.

Casting her mind back, she remembered her father mentioning how busy and crazy the docks were every day. With thousands of ships coming into the harbour AND docks carrying everything you could imagine. Then her father would comment on how strange it was that you could never hear the waves because of the shouting of orders and everything else.

She smiled as she remembered her father. A lot of people she worked for shunned her for coming from a family of dockers. The lowest of the low. Commoners to the core. But Hellen just wanted to whack these people with her stick. She was a proud docker. Her father always said being a docker was the best job.

Hellen didn't know if she agreed with him on that but being a docker wasn't a bad job. It kept her family alive and well.

A loud crash of a wave in the distance made Hellen focus back on the ugly warehouses. The killer had to be here. This was where he lived. At least when she had tracked him down the first time, and this was his only option for a hideout.

From the eccentric (to put it nicely) Lady Serpentine running the underground caves to the Queen redeveloping all unused land. This was the only place left where no one would come looking.

Hellen had to smile at herself then. She had worked it all out and tracked the killer where all those posh annoying snobs couldn't. Sometimes Hellen really wanted to whack them with her stick to shut them up. Then she reminded herself she needed to find him first.

A small deep laugh echoed around the little circle of warehouses.

Hellen picked up her massive stick. Ready to whack something.

Something fell from the sky.

Hellen jumped.

Something splashed against the hard gravel.

Blood spattered up her legs.

Hellen looked at the thing in front of her. It was a heart. A cleanly sliced out heart.

Touching it briefly, Hellen could still feel the warmth pulse through it. This heart was a fresh kill.

Something landed on Hellen.

Knocking her to the ground.

Hellen's face smashed into the gravel.

Slicing her head.

Pushing herself back up, she knew exactly what it was as she pushed the thing off her.

It was a corpse.

A fresh warm corpse. The fresh still-vibrant rich red blood dripped out of the many wounds. It was impossible to tell if this person was a man or woman. There were simply too many cuts and injuries. From the warm pieces of flayed skin from the legs that flapped in the gentle breeze to where all the organs had been carefully carved out from the still living victim.

A part of Hellen wanted to whack herself with

her massive stick. She was a failure. Her arrogance of thinking she was so smart to know where the killer was had made her lazy. She knew the killer was here. But instead of hunting this part of the docks high and low. Hellen simply stood there waiting for the killer to come to her.

The posh snobs wouldn't have waited. They would have searched the place. They- Hellen cut herself off. She knew thinking wasn't helpful. After all she was a Procurator, a good one. And if all that failed to make her feel good then at least she could say to people she was a best friend with the daughter of a Noble Family who was a Dominicus Procurator herself. That always made people silent and run away at parties.

Hellen bit her lip she was right about the killer being here. But she also knew the next part. Just like before, the Killer revealed his location to Hellen then the horror of this man was revealed.

Hellen's hand tightened around her massive stick making her knuckles turn white. Because unlike last time, she would stop this killer or she would die trying. Hellen couldn't go back to her Dominicus Procurator a failure.

***

After an hour of trying to find a way to the roof, Hellen had finally made it. She couldn't believe how hard it was to find a ladder. It was ridiculous. She didn't even want to think about how dock workers use to get up here for their extra… activities.

As she stepped off the ladder onto the cold hard metal rooftop, she gasped. This was beautiful. For tens upon tens of metres either side of her was nothing except dirty hard metal roofing. But the impressive part was the view.

Up here Hellen could see almost all of Ordericous, the beautiful busy harbour with tens of ships docking and unloading, the stunning castle and city in the distance and the lush forests behind her. This was beautiful. Perhaps she could bring a boy here one day for some fun.

The smell of sweat and salt reminded her of her father after a hard day's work at the dock. Then the sound of someone hitting metal made her look to her right.

In the distance, there was a black humanoid shape near the edge, presumably close to where she was standing below earlier.

Sweat dripped down her back and forehead. All her skin turned cold and numb. Her knuckles went white gripping her massive stick. She wanted to whack something.

Walking towards the black humanoid shape, Hellen had to fight herself to keep her mind focused. What if the Killer took her?

What if the Killer attacked her?

What if-

Hellen focused herself to stop. It was all useless. If her best friend Alessandria Fireheart had taught her anything, it was the importance of staying calm. As much as Hellen just wanted to whack people over the head, Alessandria might have a point in this case.

To force her mind off the Killer, Hellen focused on the hard metal roofing that banged and creeped with every step.

There was a shard of rusty metal on the ground.

Not sure if the Killer was watching her, she grabbed it. Sliding it into her pocket.

The smell of sweat and salt from earlier become faint. Being replaced with her own fear and the smell of rotten meat.

As she got closer to the black humanoid shape, Hellen could start to make out it was a man dressed in black leather. Holding something long and silver dripping dark red liquid.

She needed to be prepared but Hellen wanted to run.

She wanted to run away and never see this man.

Hellen remembered the horrors of seeing this man kill before. Her own fear back then had stopped her from arresting this deranged Killer. She was not going to let that happen again.

When Hellen was only a few metres away from him, she stopped. This Killer was disgusting. The black leather was no normal leather. It was human leather. Made from the freshly flayed skin of his victims. It lovingly hugged his strong muscular frame.

As she suspected this foul Killer was holding a long sharp sword dripping blood in one hand. But in the other hand, he was holding a strange dagger that glowed bright red at her. The closer she got, the brighter it glowed.

Forcing herself to down her fear, Hellen looked at him in the eye, those massive crazy white eyes that beamed at her. Maybe he liked her flesh. He definitely wasn't the first man, but he wasn't her type.

More sweat dripped down her back.

Hellen sighed. "By the Power of the

Procuratorus, I am placing ya under arrest," she said.

The man cocked his head.

Did he not understand the words?

A weight pressed against Hellen's chest. She didn't know what to do now. Should she try and arrest him?

Slowly, Hellen started to walk over to the man. Trying to make sure she didn't make any sudden moves.

He coughed.

Hellen almost jumped but she didn't want to look weak.

Those massive crazy white eyes followed Hellen as she walked.

The bright red dagger glowed even brighter. It looked red hot.

It *was* red hot. Smoke started to pour from the foul man's hand.

He screamed.

Charging at Hellen.

She thrusted out her massive stick.

He dodged.

He slashed his sword at her.

She raised her massive stick. Before whacking him with it.

His jaw cracked briefly.

The red dagger flashed.

A magical wave of energy threw Hellen to the ground.

Her face smashed into the rusty metal roofing.

The man jumped into the air.

Hellen whacked him again.

He went flying.

He landed with a thud. Denting the roof.
Those massive crazy eyes opened even wider.
The dagger started glowing again.
Screaming the man charged at Hellen.
His sword swirled and twirled rapidly in the air.
Hellen tried to dodge all the attacks.
He was too quick.
He sliced her hand deep.
Dark red blood poured out.
The Killer screamed in utter delight.
Hellen went to cover her hand.
He slashed at her again.
Hellen tried to block.
The Killer grabbed her massive stick. Pulling hard.
Pain flooded Hellen's sliced hand.
She released.
The man punched her.
Her other hand let go.
The Killer threw her massive stick off the roof.
Hellen's body filled with rage.
How dare he.
She charged at him.
Punching and kicking.
The Killer was quick.
Perfectly dodging each attack.
The dagger glowed red hot once again.
A magical wave threw Hellen to the edge of the roof.
Hellen saw the ground tens of metres below.
She tried to keep her balance.
The man pushed her over.

Hellen grabbed onto the edge of the roof.

Her fingers hating the feel of the cold sharp metal.

Her knuckles ghostly white as she clung to the edge.

Her mind raced.

Was she going to die?

Would she fall?

After a few moments, the disgusting Killer stepped over the edge of the warehouse. Only a few centimetres away from Hellen's hands. Looking out over Ordericous. Almost admiring the view. The arrogant little so and so.

Hellen wanted to grab those foul human leather legs and pull him over the edge. But she knew she wasn't strong enough. He needed to be weakened first.

Those massive crazy white eyes looked down on her. Hellen wanted to rip them out.

He smiled. "Ya that one. The one tried to stop me. The Procurator that hide when I played with that person. Ya could have come out to play. I love a play mate. That blood and meat was delicious. Ya should have tried some,"

A part of Hellen wanted to let go. She didn't want to listen to this. But she had her duty to do.

"You will never win. If ya kill me-"

"I don't want to kill ya. I want a play mate. I want to have fun with ya. If not, I'll get ya body and chop ya up,"

Those crazy eyes almost lit up at the thought.

Hellen's heart raced.

"Won't that spoil my flavour?"

The Killer paused for a moment. Looking up

at the sky.

She needed to think.

"Na," the man said.

He raised his foot to stamp on her hands.

Hellen didn't want to die.

She whipped out the rusty metal shard.

She thrusted it into the man's other leg.

He screamed.

Those crazy white eyes shutting in pain.

He started to fall towards the edge.

Hellen grabbed him. Throwing him off the roof.

The sound of smashing bones and spattering blood echoed behind her.

***

Looking at the pile of smashed up flesh, bones and brain matter in front of her, Hellen couldn't help but smile.

As she felt the rough gravel beneath her booted feet and heard the shouting of men in the distance with the gentle crashing of the waves too. Hellen knew she had completed her duty and completed her mission. That's all she ever wanted. Well that and some special fun.

Looking over at the warehouses around her with their ugly metal cladding, she knew this place was condemned and soon would be redeveped by the Queen. Maybe that was a good thing. It might help erase this monster's legacy.

With her massive stick that she found closer to the pile of flesh, Hellen whacked the human leather for no particular reason. Except now she could say she had successfully whacked him more than once or twice. And in her experience, it was always good to make sure the criminal was dead.

Breathing in the salty air from the nearby sea made Hellen pause. Her work today was of course small in the grand scheme of things, but she had made a difference. At least this would never happen again.

GET YOUR FREE AND EXCLUSIVE SHORT STORY NOW! LEARN ABOUT NEMESIO'S PAST!

https://www.subscribepage.com/fireheart

Thank you for reading.

I hoped you enjoyed it.

If you want a FREE book and keep up to date about new books and project. Then please sign up for my newsletter at www.connorwhiteley.net/

Have a great day.

About the author:

Connor Whiteley is the author of over 30 books in the sci-fi fantasy, nonfiction psychology and books for writer's genre and he is a Human Branding Speaker and Consultant.

He is a passionate warhammer 40,000 reader, psychology student and author.

Who narrates his own audiobooks and he hosts The Psychology World Podcast.

All whilst studying Psychology at the University of Kent, England.

Also, he was a former Explorer Scout where he gave a speech to the Maltese President in August 2018 and he attended Prince Charles' 70th Birthday Party at Buckingham Palace in May 2018.

Plus, he is a self-confessed coffee lover!

OTHER SHORT STORIES BY CONNOR WHITELEY

Blade of The Emperor

Arbiter's Truth

The Bloodied Rose

Asmodia's Wrath

Heart of A Killer

Emissary of Blood

Computation of Battle

Old One's Wrath

Other books by Connor Whiteley:

The Fireheart Fantasy Series

Heart of Fire

Heart of Lies

More Coming Soon!

The Garro Series- Fantasy/Sci-fi

GARRO: GALAXY'S END

GARRO: RISE OF THE ORDER

GARRO: END TIMES

GARRO: SHORT STORIES

GARRO: COLLECTION

GARRO: HERESY

GARRO: FAITHLESS

GARRO: DESTROYER OF WORLDS

GARRO: COLLECTIONS BOOK 4-6

GARRO: MISTRESS OF BLOOD

GARRO: BEACON OF HOPE

CONNOR WHITELEY

GARRO: END OF DAYS

<u>Winter Series- Fantasy Trilogy Books</u>

WINTER'S COMING

WINTER'S HUNT

WINTER'S REVENGE

WINTER'S DISSENSION

<u>Miscellaneous:</u>

THE ANGEL OF RETURN

THE ANGEL OF FREEDOM

All books in 'An Introductory Series':

BIOLOGICAL PSYCHOLOGY 3RD EDITION

COGNITIVE PSYCHOLOGY THIRD EDITION

SOCIAL PSYCHOLOGY- 3RD EDITION

ABNORMAL PSYCHOLOGY 3RD EDITION

PSYCHOLOGY OF RELATIONSHIPS- 3RD EDITION

DEVELOPMENTAL PSYCHOLOGY 3RD EDITION

HEALTH PSYCHOLOGY

RESEARCH IN PSYCHOLOGY

A GUIDE TO MENTAL HEALTH AND TREATMENT AROUND THE WORLD- A GLOBAL LOOK AT DEPRESSION

FORENSIC PSYCHOLOGY

THE FORENSIC PSYCHOLOGY OF THEFT, BURGLARY AND OTHER

RIMES AGAINST PROPERTY

CRIMINAL PROFILING: A FORENSIC PSYCHOLOGY GUIDE TO FBI PROFILING AND GEOGRAPHICAL AND STATISTICAL PROFILING.

CLINICAL PSYCHOLOGY

FORMULATION IN PSYCHOTHERAPY

Companion guides:

<u>BIOLOGICAL PSYCHOLOGY 2ND EDITION WORKBOOK</u>

<u>COGNITIVE PSYCHOLOGY 2ND EDITION WORKBOOK</u>

<u>SOCIOCULTURAL PSYCHOLOGY 2ND EDITION WORKBOOK</u>

<u>ABNORMAL PSYCHOLOGY 2ND EDITION WORKBOOK</u>

<u>PSYCHOLOGY OF HUMAN RELATIONSHIPS 2ND EDITION WORKBOOK</u>

<u>HEALTH PSYCHOLOGY WORKBOOK</u>

<u>FORENSIC PSYCHOLOGY WORKBOOK</u>

Audiobooks by Connor Whiteley:

BIOLOGICAL PSYCHOLOGY

COGNITIVE PSYCHOLOGY

SOCIOCULTURAL PSYCHOLOGY

ABNORMAL PSYCHOLOGY

PSYCHOLOGY OF HUMAN RELATIONSHIPS

HEALTH PSYCHOLOGY

DEVELOPMENTAL PSYCHOLOGY

RESEARCH IN PSYCHOLOGY

FORENSIC PSYCHOLOGY

GARRO: GALAXY'S END

GARRO: RISE OF THE ORDER

GARRO: SHORT STORIES

GARRO: END TIMES

GARRO: COLLECTION

GARRO: HERESY

GARRO: FAITHLESS

GARRO: DESTROYER OF WORLDS

GARRO: COLLECTION BOOKS 4-6

GARRO: COLLECTION BOOKS 1-6

Business books:

TIME MANAGEMENT: A GUIDE FOR STUDENTS AND WORKERS

LEADERSHIP: WHAT MAKES A GOOD LEADER? A GUIDE FOR STUDENTS AND WORKERS.

BUSINESS SKILLS: HOW TO SURVIVE THE BUSINESS WORLD? A GUIDE FOR STUDENTS, EMPLOYEES AND EMPLOYERS.

BUSINESS COLLECTION

GET YOUR FREE BOOK AT:
WWW.CONNORWHITELEY.NET

www.ingramcontent.com/pod-product-compliance
Lightning Source LLC
LaVergne TN
LVHW011901060526
838200LV00054B/4466